It's all one big poem for Geoff Peterson. And every stanza, check that, every *line*, packs a wallop. Yet the whole is greater than the sum of such parts. The main effect is serious and funny. Also sexy. Intensely.

--Chuck Joy
author, *How to Feel*

Gut deep & penis heavy. Raise the flag & bow from the waist, a new country has cooled from the flames. I'll bet you didn't know men talked this way to anyone.

--Sharon Dolan, author/artist
Tasmania

Geoff Peterson has remained off radar for years. I should know; try running a background check on the guy. In the words of any critic who's written a review in the last ten years: *Clearly an astonishing work of a master.*

--Madam Nhu
shred before dying

Drama & Desire jumps like the adventures of Don Quixote in Hiroshima. Peterson arranges an explosion of hypertext along with quirky structural experimentation & linguistic musings.

--Dr. Sally LeVan, Professor of English
Gannon University

DRAMA & DESIRE

texts & commentaries

Geoff Peterson

authorHOUSE

AuthorHouse™
1663 Liberty Drive, Suite 200
Bloomington, IN 47403
www.authorhouse.com
Phone: 1-800-839-8640

© 2009 Geoff Peterson. All rights reserved.

No part of this book may be reproduced, stored in a retrieval system, or transmitted by any means without the written permission of the author.

First published by AuthorHouse 3/3/2009

ISBN: 978-1-4389-5196-6 (sc)

Printed in the United States of America
Bloomington, Indiana

This book is printed on acid-free paper.

Cover photo: "Masque-no" by Rama (adapted from wikipedia.com)

Cover design: Shaun & Cornelia Abata

for Gertrude Marie

1922-2008

Other books by Geoff Peterson

Cordes Junction (1987)
Medicine Dog (1989)
Hecho en Mexico (1995)
Bad Trades (2000)
Cold Reading (2007)
Crazy Stairs (2008)

The foldings of a book...form a tomb
for our souls.

> Stephane Mallarme

The rare desires shine in constellation

> Charles Baudelaire

15/02/08
san francisco

the exhibit at the asian museum features paintings of
      the floating world 1690-1850

ukiyo-e: block prints of brothels & the kabuki theatre
in edo japan

yoshiwara its pleasure dome, to which
all points on the compass aim
said the poet

the 1st thing you notice   a hokusai lantern
and the words of ono no komachi
my heart is truly made new with desire

thus the title: *drama*
& desire

now if two words ever existed that described my life
it's those

in fact, take the dust from one & the leaf
of the other, and brew slowly
oh yes, my whole life

asuko, where buddhism landed 1300 years ago
moved to paris to be alone
and to think clearly

hougaku she wrote: direction, a point
on the compass; bearings

immersed in west african studies, she plans to return
to senegal and take up with a family
of sufi saints

here i take up
her pen given me to replace the one
i lost & notebook she gave me
to write honorably

her eyelashes, i wrote, *so black they're blue
crows rave in 3's, often*

walking at night recalls how alone i can ever know
loneliness just awareness *sans* witnesses
someone said

pigeons moaning like a dead battery

asuko at the airport nurses a drink & underlines
mallarme in french

brushes her hair & logs frequent flyer miles on 3 airlines
    alive to a new century she makes love to the fantasy
    of a normal life

and issues long scrolls of distress with her silk tongue

as a *sensei* of literature i knew the risks
the music, books & film of our story
shaped to popular tastes

i only regret the anger of those months
against myself   knowing better   and still
powerless to stand back

the thing i wanted to happen in this life didn't
until

i seem to recall the character *muchu*
"fogbound" everywhere at once
the spirit's passage through death
is dark, esp. with no one left
to pray, wrote zeami

into the mouth of my mother, b. 1925
d. 1958 *aman dei pelicula*
says the headstone

muchu can be interpreted as "rapturous
ecstasy" sd asuko referring
to her own death
stepping from the bath at nara

i dread going back to my country unchanged
except a haircut

as a ghost in the repertoire i desired to fly above my fate
      to find it in a panic or altered by hazard
      instead i enter the past

& call men younger than myself "sir"

asuko: how often do you want sex
sensei: every day, no exception
asuko: ah, such healthy

        dokusan:
        zen interview

a chinese sage once prescribed 1 ejaculation per week
for men over 50

uttered by a man who jacked off once during his entire
adolescence

on the other hand devotees of orgasm are many
& conjure romps in the courtyard
select men & women like off-shore oil esp. juicy

estimated distance of semen thrown in my life
enough to hit the moon

asuko suggests i write a book about that
a memoir: my life in search of
ecstasy, or for that matter
oblivion

smoking in bed the femme fatale—*ayame*
for my benefit, refers to priceless *shunga*
erotic scrolls showing samurai with big cocks

mounting courtesans without sweat   asuko's hard
buttocks against my belly, her slim hands taking turns
gonging my balls, her mouth silvery
like money

asuko's book of artists contains actors, poets, calligraphers, geisha, drummers, designers & boatwrights

photographed in studios & courtyards or locked into focus with flamboyant scrolls of *shodo*

each in order of rank after the emporer and regional gods going back to fire

ise, kamo, kasuga, ka-shima, mi-shima, suwa, atsu-ta & iwa-shimizu in kimono or suits & print dresses from the 50s

the text in kanji having started at the back, i require asuko's guidance   she asks that i take my time & concentrate on the fingers

in one photo a poet smokes while his wife prepares tea
in another the road to recovery is curious
& requires sustained practice

of the weavers & potters notice a fierce attention to materials their mouths dabbed with cigarettes & eyes magnified by ground lens

excellence
is in finding the imperfection
interesting

i can't help but marvel
that after so many examples i need assurance that such a life is possible

a scorpion half my age and resigned to a rogue karma
not to mention you put us on a bare stage
and we fight

calling herself a buddhist: 1ˢᵗ mistake
in the words i can't remember if
yesterday or half a life ago
i read it: why

does the monk wear out his sandals seeking
the buddha
            there is no buddha no dharma
no enlightenment within or without
says the record of lin-chi
                      kitsu! clap
of thunder   zen's post-doctorate *fuck you*
now what have you to say

but when it's good   oh man the evenings she cooks
the mornings i bring her coffee in bed—
we understand death

& sex more than no parking zones & what to buy for
        birthdays
but hard pounding doggy style (bakku)
& cries of *iku iku* "i come i come—"
followed by a profound shudder
after a rain

once at night she awoke with a cry and said she loved
        me, no *really*

it's okay i sd like it was just a bad dream

she's 29 & ancient
she's japanese
& speaks 5 languages
she's got a place in gifu
& one in paris
and she's got friends
in publishing

any questions

the missed call on my cell phone says *unknown*
that's asuko tonight across the pacific
as unknown as you can get

almost a year without touching   *please you're my last
     chance at love i know i have made
mistakes*

reading tanizaki's *naomi* i am reminded
it doesn't get any better for an old man
than holding a young woman
asleep on his chest

like *lolita* in translation—at the toilet
i flush   in the mirror   *tu t'es pas regarde
you,* do you see it   who she called
when she called you

i haven't said in so many words but it's snowing in gifu

this séance of days—at work on the poem as flat
as the bile-green shingles on an outhouse roof
(see what I mean)

not one good shit since they stole the election
i'm tired of being alone—*bound but not
gagged* i wrote with a pen left on the table

asuko, jump start the words   loose the tiger
in my balls & make me hungry
recall the pacific clipper when i roared
into town and opened wounds for all to see
then disappeared

i have always known the end was out there
like the rainy season   so early this year
by june she'll be on a ward where her mother
works graveyards

and i'll fly with her money from a swiss account
& the cat in a cage   and one golden afternoon
she'll admit she's been sent with a message
from my mother

it's not that i'm eager to die, she says, *but few things are*
    worth surviving

this fall i'll enter a monastery and give away my books
i will unfurl my life in a endless scroll with all
the fruits of my heart, bruised as they are
& go to mexico

i will go to plum village
in the pyrenees
& weep

remind me to email asuko requesting a japanese
"script"   *if i meet yr mother*

my gift an illustrated dialogue
between an american & japanese
about losing husbands

to show her mother i am not a stranger
to loss   & asuko ponders
my motives

i have told myself i am with a woman
with designs to improve her english

i watch her tug on my ring finger without success
turquoise & silver of the navaho
in marriage to myself

you don't want to marry me she pouts
i remind her i don't wish to marry anyone
but will in an emergency

thus i buy a duplicate she wears around her neck
featured in rare photos of her—always
shy & barely in focus

In just a minute
I made my reputation.
On my face as I look back,
the snow is falling.
Is this our parting?

        --Nakamura Utaeman III
          Kabuki actor

Stephane Mallarme (1842-1898)

Il a publie quelque poemes dans le Pamasse contemporain de 1866, une scene d'*Herodiade* (1871) et *l'Apris-midi d'un faune* (1876), lorsque son eloge par Huysmans, dans le roman *A rebouts*, lui apporte brusquement la celebrite. Son poeme "Un coup de des jamais n'abolira le hazard" (1897) forme premier movement de son projet de "livre" absolu. Son oeuvre, malgre sa brievete et son inachevement, a ete determinante poue l'evolution de la literature au cours du xx es.

transcribed from website
by asuko, 08/06

late in spring i walk around the city and watch the light
 fade from windows

i am not alone   a downtown campus offers night
 studies
in mallarme   flags on buildings hang limp
in the haze   & a man pours pernod
from an ancient cellar

there is barely a sound
but a flute in my temporal lobe

i want to tell a woman six thousand miles away i love her
 all out of proportion

but my calls fail and all i can do is stop trying

asuko's calling me by her name for me   *sensei*
makes me real to be that a teacher sometimes i even
want to be

but i've got to be who i am, not a person in the strict sense
but the shadow i married at the beginning—alone &
without shame

mairu: to be beaten; to be struck (by a girl's charm)

they said i'd meet her over there
that i'd not come back   they sd
i'd meet her like a life-long riddle
finally solved   they sd i
deserted them & it was about time

my voices

suddenly there's not enough history to explain my life

one year later say the movie titles   what good comes
from mowing lawns in erie pa. a man cannot write in his
father's house   but must feel reckless to start

back & forth in rows i conjure acts too terrible to structure
ghost-fucks

with wives who sell their golden purses for a column inch
in the paper   i invite them in the spirit of adventure &
the wish for annihilation

if you didn't come out of the period between hiroshima
        & korea you have no idea

all those trust fund mutants teaching english
to textile workers in kowloon who say
actually or its cognates
then fly home with stories about pollution
& prejudice against women

bronze kids from santa barbara bound
for delhi, wage scabs for jesus
or some bodhisattva

asuko refuses to acknowledge my fury   you bark she
        says & cites my birth in the year of the dog as why
        she's come a dragon

bow wow, bitch   maybe i'm not making sense but
i have paid my dues to be crazy

you can spot americans not by swagger but nonchalance:
we are the movie we imagine

(watching brando in *sayonara,* or me
anywhere) check out these jive ass *gaijin* with street
    hustles for halos and their cruise control in the
    world

to notice strangers as sedate forms of mayhem but never
    to stop doing what we're doing

america the mask inside you to get through the lonely
    hours to get through the lonely hours beside her
    oh forget i said that

for our 1st night on rue charlemagne i explain i'm pushing
    60 and dying

you're not dying, she laughs, you're right here inside *me*
    we're *both* dying

she not yet 30.   i've explained to her
my desire to throw my life down a flight of stairs (the
    subject of another book) to see what happens

i also will throw *my* life, she argues complaining of fatigue
    i offer a petit massage and watch 1 good thing lead
    to another

recalling that line of rimbaud's: "her poor eyelids
fluttered under my lips"   *tu ete tres gentil*
she whispers   in a sense i am as yet
unfamiliar with, i.e. noble

naked in the cold light we shower, curious i am not erect
    to see her   in bed demonstrate a technique for
    installing a condom
        japan
make best *gomu,* she boasts—but too small for you
bite is *deek*, she asks
oui

migoto she breathes upon it (fine, splendid, admirable)

by the 2nd night we abandon all precaution   *yatte,* she
    gasps:
more   *hageshiku*: harder
hayaku: faster

my professional says when i fall in love it must be
	excruciating let me tell you

sobbing i don't understand the sadness that life is slipping
	away in espana, morocco, tunis at the hotel arles

being debriefed before this can happen   the journey's
meaning

says the poem stands as a monument to misery
beginning at the vacant apartment of a girl 1 day older
due to an imaginary line under water

all morning i keep seeing our lady in the back of
limousines   at notre dame a stranger cries, blows his
nose genuflects & leaves

all funerals make me horny   slip the man's widow
into black pants, or fly in the crazy sister
from sacramento

& you have the etymology of *debauche*

that's why the poem describes asuko as not a goddess
but an apparition   woman as root expression
of yr separation from place
& its healing

i have determined not to stay for the mass of the
	faithful
but to walk the philosopher's walk in the rain
and all that life otherwise

in kyoto the pond houses ducks and a mossy boat
and a shack i'd like to live in

i explain all places have a line shack at the lower or
          higher
levels depending, and provide hay for the horses

moving upward or down depending is hard work
at night in yr sleep

asuko invites me not to stop for the night but to inhabit
a version of myself higher or lower depending

this is why i search for a bathroom to be alone

let me get this straight   she wants me to kneel
seiza style in the temple with inkstone & brush
and copy the diamond sutra in kanji

then stagger forward and submit it before
tossing coins in a grate—and for that i paid ¥600
so that this winter a monk can laugh his ass off

copy that.

i will travel alone i will stay away   days, months
& rent a cabin in the woods and call you
to send money

there will never be enough money
sometimes you will be left to eat alone
& asked that we fight cleanly

we've already talked about sex& birth control
you prefer *kijoi* (on top) & *gammen kijo*
(sitting on face) you told me

i have to go to bed so we can have this talk
before dawn i'll sleep in the car

on 2nd thought i'm having difficulty being here
please—

stop to consider perhaps i am not the man
to fulfill yr phantom needs

asuko calls at 3 a.m. pacific time to complain about my
 poems & argue about changing her name   before
 we marry she says
she'll consult a lawyer about a contract regarding my
 work

she says i am ruthless in gutting relationships for the
 purpose of disclosure not to mention the notices
 for another book

i think of the word *self-serving* in all its implications

i tell her it's true it's not the entire story but
let it stand as a noteworthy contribution
to the research

i wish i could accommodate her wishes on this matter
but there's nothing to say really   goodbye   *have a good
 life*

pause. *i don't know what to say*

say goodbye

all right then & hangs up

next i gut my apartment burn my clothes drive to a
 monastery & turn myself in

asuko & i in flight means close calls on freeways
in other people's cars
we'll enter the desert on foot

just when we think it's clear they've given up
transmission's interrupted—
headlights appear

we have to push ourselves to keep moving if we can
    just
make it over this mountain we'll reach cover, food &
    water

halfway up we spot the first motorcycle's dust
followed by assault vehicles & freeze
like lumps of coal

maybe they'll take us for rocks or pieces of garbage
instead we're handcuffed in back of a rover but refuse
to answer questions without a lawyer

lately we dare not look at each other
but instead get used to the idea we're alone

...living only for the moment, turning our full attention to the pleasures of the moon, the snow, the cherry blossoms, and the maple leaves; singing songs, drinking wine, diverting ourselves in just floating, floating; caring not a whit for the pauperism staring us in the face, refusing to be disheartened, like a gourd floating along the river current: this is what we call the floating world....

from *Drama & Desire*, 2008

rain all night in gifu   coil
of incense   asuko's crowded notes
& my practice breathing in my underwear

while bamboo sways about the house
if they're right and the western horizon
is paradise, this is it

startled by thunder   before it breaks you can smell it
the rain   its sheets sweeping the leaves
in updrafts

makes you wonder how much you notice with age
makes you bow to preserve it
rain, trees & inland sea

it's from these the rest comes   affection
for family, friends, desire for sex
& *kitsu*

the privilege to abandon all

asuko's suitcase is so light there must be a mistake
according to immigration

rain, she argues. but you cannot bring rain
into the country, citing

the secret collected letters   children's writing
as a crusade   on the plane she sorts them

velvet bags in rows tied with a twist
like eggs

they're letters from school kids to kids all over
peace letters to the world

peace being sweeter than justice   better
than each letter going unsigned

heiwa: "a fierce peace, a fierce peace
& a sense of the world," goes the aria*

peace letters, i sd
realizing at once how perfect she was for the job

*from the opera *Dr. Atomic*, Peter Sellars, libretto

since soaking at the hot springs 72 hrs pass
without speaking   i sleep i watch tv
i place an order for eggs & seaweed

before bathing we wash our hair and soap each other
with both hands   anus pink & squeaky
my shaft against her belly

on the 3rd night we wade deep into psychic debt
to her mother   as long as she shall live
is my karma, she explains

ni sakarau means not to disobey, offend
or oppose, esp. as the older daughter
is japanese custom

we argue because her mother is a snake
whose venom poisons our future
thus i grow faint & weary

afterwards she reads our horoscope
in francaise   expect an intense year, it says
dramatic shift of emphasis

suggests medical problems in october
forget my mother—*fais-moi l'amour*, she begs
we make baby before you die

of one man's paris, i sing   fractured ceramic tiles
feature a woman of course & includes
goodbye in all its forms

so that we can get past all that at the start

asuko inquires what is meant by "floating world" as i've
outlined it   searching for words as witness
to my smoky heart i behold change
sea change at depth

not merely her expression (*kao*) but her entire mask
shifts: 1st a haunted ingenue & then others—
japanese, some eurasian....

omote, shaved eyebrows
& blackened teeth: gateway
to another world where we both exist
& non-exist as lovers

on the inside the rough primitive crawl space
of the psyche
vengeful ghosts, pearly & cherry lipped
the eyes lit from elsewhere

i narrate my travels
in time lapse: a month alone on trains, cafes & hotels
notebooks filled with panic
je suis perdu

i don't take photos but process place
as meditation   woman
vortex   void
& seek my ghosts in traffic   thus we walk
and catalog writers she loves who are translated
in the west: mishima of course but
unexpected is her degree of reverence

for *seppuku*
 followed by gossip
about yoko ono & the fabulous wealth of families
back home

at charles de gaulle i pass through security & buy a
    copy
of *le petit prince* for my daughter
c'est de rigeur, nez pas   americans
must depart with a fascist fantasy
in their luggage

reminds me of sartre in the 60s   *les americains*
i love them because they persist in buying
le nausee

was it *being & nothingness*—or did i just make that up

every *petite fille* with black hair
from behind might just be....   if she turns around
asian it stuns me

at place st. michel she sd if i miss my flight or change
my mind to call her   but i'm american
& *j'ai la diarrhee*

asuko stop me   i thought i wasn't being honest
but now i don't know what i know
je ne peux plus me passer de toi
i cannot live without you
signed, *un homme*

always the dream to attain purity   as in the pure land
      sect or to see clearly like zen

maybe that's what asuko means when she calls happiness
      an illusion

there are moments i have said in the depths of myself,
      yes this is hell or *now i am in hell*

and what is hell but illusion of my mind attached to her
      body & will change and clarity be restored

i must live this out despite what i know, but live with tall
      buildings in recognition of light

such is the story i've told myself in my wisdom
to feather my bed in hell

p.s. every time i was in hell i wasn't—
just a growth spurt says the staff at the clinic

one year ago today
i left her house in gifu
and loosened my bowels

now i live in a friend's garage
and watch it rain in the open door
the wind is ravishing

the fact that i can neither speak to her in french
nor in japanese
makes me indigent

the fact that i can sit at dinner over a glass
of cabernet & intone: *alors*
makes me adorable

asuko goes to a "friend's" apartment in the 6th arr.
for her clothes and can't find a cab because
it's sunday

and i'm wondering how long it takes when the key
 turns
in the lock—i love *you*
she cries, i want to *be* with you
i always be alone   i'm tired   i feel
you protect my heart

leaving me no choice but to grab her arms
& recount *madama butterfly* as deranged euro
fantasy, thank you

not to mention brando in *sayonara*—merely
puccini with a happy ending
which leads to our agreeing to respect
artists without money

analysis of *hiroshima mon amour*
or chopin at st. julien-le-pauve
by a pianist named junko
leaves her desolate

but reminds her of an interview with godard
she conducted on behalf—   *wait*
*—an interview with jean-luc godard
in person*

montage: make love/ fall asleep/ awake it's raining/
 asleep on her stomach/ what i've learned is less
 than a footnote/ and for that we're all
empty modern people stumbling in our spirit world

asuko's taught me anything's possible—i told her
that—anything, & not to hesitate
as desire is a dog on fire

and she sd what she learned
from me are some dirty words in english
& things about writing

in rm 18 at the hotel esmeralda the wall paper's sick
with flowers, even the ceiling is laden

la fenetre above the river, a pink table & a scarlet lamp
beside a woman's voice in the chair

monet painted this place
see it at the musee d'orsay noon to 8 weekdays

with an artist's pencil what's not possible he said
even love with a girl in a café

hugo lived here when he wrote *hunchback*   i can see him
          brooding behind quasimodo's gnarled mask

no matter what happens
there will always be that—even if it's not true

& she no more than a rumor on a twisted staircase

she cannot help herself   *je suis fatigue* she says,
   applying antibiotic to her rashes she can never
   wear makeup

3 months in mali
six in senegal interviewing brothers of islamic
couvades for a thesis

life-flighted—dakar to hotel dieu:
iv's on drip, then weeks
underlining pages in *les fantoms afrique*
untranslated into english

3 months later
undressed she comes to me a crooked stick
the ruins of asuko the daughter
of takahashi, son of a magistrate
i am what's left, she says
meaning me

alone i rifle her drawers & find a double A
battery, one paper clip
all she owns of this hemisphere in a carry-on

finally i have met the woman whose life is the one
i always dreamt for myself

her   1ˢᵗ   memory: walking   to   the   hospital   with   her
         mother
to have her sister
                          a year later her father lay dead

liver failure at 40
everyone drink alcohol, she says
he a lawyer   his choice

to stay at the apartment to play with her
asuko will turn three when informed
1 year later it hits her   death
                             as *forever* induces coma
that lasts a year   no, two   for which she will live
& breathe somewhere not
of this world

hospitalized & fed
through a tube she travels
the vital circuits backwards, transactions
with balloon payments that promise at least
survival in another life

soon she will tell of her 1ˢᵗ job teaching
on okinawa   but stops

we are both athletes of the heart, i remind her
besides

i've been to that island in my dreams (see
my okinawa poems) so there need
be nothing held back

she says she can't right now
but you will—some day
she says she does not believe in psychology

what i feel when i touch the marble head of mary
by geoff peterson:
                   where is god
calling from   my empty bones my mother

elsewhere
between my fingers as i write this
in the chapel at lisieux

her illness & death a long corridor of snow
candle-lit by desire
to drift above the lights of my town
into pure horror

i no longer tire of waiting   my whole life
a shadow lengthening to flame

now in japan
concluding the o-ban i launch the paper boat
and pray:

what can i do to bring you back
her answer: nothing

Zeami (1363-1443) says:

a bad play which one can make something of
by taking advantage of its defects
& "breaking one's bones" in the acting....

i am thinking on these & sundry quotes
while trying to replay my sex
with asuko for the 99th time
                                how she comes
appearing as herself
from the pines
on boards above the gentle tide
the shinto red *torii* reflected in the lapping

in the noh drama it is said some roles
are so arduous they shorten the actor's life

but it's what i feel holding her tiny
beating heart against me
i argue

what is it about the mystery that attracts
the west but
a ghost story

in the words of famed sinologist arthur waley
quell métier!

*But I ask you to look at the wooden puppets
worn out by their moment of play onstage!*
                              Han shan, Cold Mountain

before my birth this time i decided
my mission was to work out
my problems with women

mother dead at 33
2 marriages
1 abortion later
a litany of disappointments culminating
in suicide—not mine, hers

love suicides, chikamatsu called them
manning his fierce puppets
in furious pantomime

drama: n. *dorama,* a play, but also drama of off-stage
as in *sturm und drang* or better yet
"drama queen"

desire: n. *yokubo*, as craving; lust, greed, esp. given to
obsession in the form of madness
in short, life

asuko & i compare breast size and mine
are larger

but since we've become lovers she says
hers have ripened   & her stomach

concave and pelvis acute angles & valleys
stick-like translucent thighs

after work she meets me wearing the mask
of meaning business

in the noh i remind her
some masks are national treasures

power jacket, black turtleneck &
pressed slacks, boots

black shiny hair pulled back, no
makeup or jewely, unearthly flesh

fantome of the psychic network
dressed to kill

and i tease her because i want to fuck her
in her transcendent medium

but she's annoyed because she believes
she is who she's dressed up to be

and that must always be someone not quite
but on her way here

Minamoto no Shigeyuki (d. 1000)

Kaze wo itami   Whipped by a fierce wind
Iwa utsu nami no   And dashed like the ocean waves
Onore no mi   Against the rocks—
Kudakete mono wo   I alone am broken to bits
Omou koro kana   And now am lost in longing.

           translated by donald keene

i don't know what i was thinking
is longing the most
extreme degree of loneliness
if so, move over buddy
you're not alone

35 years ago i swam to this island
to walk on the beach and meet a radio operator
with an accent

put the woman on the ship he instructed
& slapped a mosquito
then get back here

today i sunbathe on an american tomb
10,000 miles away
& doze with a book by no known author

in the text asuko drives me in a rented car
to visit a shrine that honors spirits
of the most wretched dead

i hear buoys rocking far out in the channel
but when i awake the sky is blank
and my hands smell of gas

asuko in italy with her mother years before either knew
they would loathe each other
said

she read dante's *la vita nuova* despite having problems
with the language and finding his sonnettos
incomprehensible

i could quote cavalcante's sonnet to his friend chiding
    him on his behavior following the death of beatrice
    but

i'd rather not   so let me remind her of the great lesson
in reading dante and why *e miglior fabbro* is a force

repeat after me
never fuck with a poet—he always has the last word
capisce

don't forget to mention after we broke up i forget which
      time asuko sd

her grandfather the honorable judge was right
"he warned me about americans"
& not to waste her time

today "if i saw an american dying in the street
i would not stoop to help"
                                  i recognize it
as scripture to be kept a secret to be taken out & dusted
      like a vase from the ancient period when the world
      was water

for asuko it's a case of original mind
& membership in the big club
nihon's shadow islands

wisely it serves a certain beauty on the face
of postcards about the floating world
everyone's got their brand
of fascism

all it takes is a gnarly *gaijin* to incite it   in fact

100 nights of writing goodbye begins to peel back
the layers of dread i locked away
before the altar of marriage
& state sponsored nihilism

such is to know war in the bones of the structure

on our last night in paris we bathe together
she asks would i love her more if she understood
english perfectly

figure a 30-40% comprehension rate (a generous
estimate) of everything i say
and do, maybe

i assure her not only is it unnecessary but i prefer
the breakdown of language as the mode of transit
before us

the certainty of being understood is not what drives us
so let us not rely on words and choose instead
fishy silence

i am the eel (*unagi*) and she the cave
quoting the ancient legend
exactly

from the hypocenter above the river ota we shove off
into the current bound for miyajima

6 hrs in the a-bomb museum at hiroshima
induces radiation sickness
i log: empathy, n. *dokan*
and ring the bell

recall new mexico: scientists locked into cubicles
like writers in hollywood
faulkner even, fitzgerald
slaves of a system

knowing in yr bones that given a set of circumstances
you forgot you created, you're capable
of anything, anything
now live with that

the ferryboat skipper volunteers to take our picture
and tries to make us laugh

the textbooks told us regarding the morality
of aug. 6 *the jury is still out*

in the photo we stare
grim faced, broken before we've begun
on the island the deer are buddhist & eat from our
      hands

asuko-san: my rabid francophile who rises at dawn
to read mallarme, now hear this

it's warm in new york—i watch a young german couple
in a deli dig each other and think
of you & me
                merci for paris—
i told my therapist it was my happiest time
don't tell me it's finished

i want to talk about the things i love
when i see you but you know
that i'm foolish

i enjoy drinking the cha you gave me
please have a pleasant flight
i hope they feed you on the plane

be sure to turn down the heat when you leave
i miss you already and smile ferociously
in traffic

p.s. remind me to explain
"dig each other"

one past life searching for her father
2 boyfriends so far in her travels
both disabled

boyfriend #1 in cameroon shooting film
et #2 with a progressive disease
that leaves you crippled

she asks if i've ever been in a fight
with men *oui*

a hater of violence it follows her everywhere
one boyfriend beating another
for conduct unbecoming

not since i've stopped going to bars i answer
we met in a bar, she reminds me
but that's another life

there is no other life she says

asuko calls at 3 a.m. to say she's alone "on the mountain"
    and it's snowing

after snow non-stop for 3 days the doors
frozen and windows sealed

i inquire if there's heat   heat there is—
& blankets & enough food & books of course

sounds delightful, i marvel   & wish i were
there   so what's the problem

no problem

i can tell by her voice this is a painful admission

i recall sex tricks we've perfected
with the aid of music on rainy afternoons
but she remains intent on literature:
it is so over between us

those eyes blaze with such brokenness
see how they release bolts of silk
& rattles of ancient coins

how can she understand i have known her
from before the beginning

in a boat i will return to shikoku in a white robe
& trace the route of kukai's 88 temples
backwards

i will offer prayers for the wrong performed
in the cause of love

like kukai i too will fast
till the skin sticks to my bones
and i glow in the moonlight

i will meet the old monk on the road
and beg to have my bowl shattered

fukuzatsu. complexity, complication

on nov 20 2006 the day before my birthday
asuko-san was denied entry
into my country

her reasons for travel determined to be
unclear, that is, suspect

applicant being detained at airport   incommunicado
until such time to be put on the next flight
back to nagoya

applicant informed it would require a visa to enter
this country ever again

posted at all ports of entry
an electronic flag beside her passport photo:
watch for this woman

24 hrs on a plane   it takes barbiturates
and 3 bottles of scotch to keep her
from going out the exit

at immigration
she could not document one place to connect her to a life
    prior to landing

which tends to arouse suspicion

of these & other matters she chose not to inform me
until later

that in paris she resigned her job & surrendered the keys
    to her apartment

that she notified her african sponsor of her not
returning due to matters of health

that she returned to japan to inform the department
chair she was withdrawing
from doctoral studies

and instead went home to live with her mother

I sd how could you do that—erase yrself
so completely   it's like you died
and she sd *maybe i did*

in the dream i reside in paris for an unspecified period
today is friday signs on every wall:
asuko's english prompts

she sits on rainy afternoons in the bedroom filled
with books in three languages and reminds me
to practice hiragana

i've just opened a letter from an american i don't know
who's buying one of my poems for the usual fee
and has enclosed two $100 bills

i have raised my voice, maybe it's the rain: *look*
you have a life here, yr job is interesting
you travel you live in paris

half the year you have interesting friends
you're going back to that
& i'm going home, *compri*

i understand she says *i'm sorry*
& holds me with our clothes on   we make love
standing   *ok* i whisper

or was it the rain   & fall into
another life—like the electric purr
of cards in a dealer's hands

meditation over water:

breathe slowly with feet on floor
release everything not me
asuko advises

who am i crossing this sheer moonlit space
to engage
but what is inside me

at the café charlatan she explained that levi-strauss
was a genius but *la pensee sauvage*
is not anthropology

yes i sd it's philosophy, paying the check

on the way back to the hotel she gripped my arm
please i don't want
to destroy you

she'd thought long & hard before saying it

(did she mean destroy me by not sharing
my language because i rely so much
on it for my work, or)

back at the room she unfastens me to behold
the object of desire in its most
present tense

she takes it by increments wholly
in the mouth vulva
liquid rich

when my hips get into it

men write sex like turning on a wind machine
i wrote
        this marvel, *oishii* (delicious)
my nose couched inside her
from behind
        fuck me says the commandment
in japanese

to come is to make lightning on her chest, her neck
cheek & hair
        toku to unfasten, discharge

the seed of islands

now permit me to touch a pearly drop to her lips
          am i not in the radiance
of kwan-lin, goddess of mercy

i watch her apply stamps to postcards written
in hiragana—left to right

originally called women's writing
the language of the greatest shower of poems
the earth has witnessed

but i am curious as to when
to write top to bottom & right to left:
when paper size is appropriate, she says

what poem i would be if the characters in her hand
were tattooed on my chest

seated on a park bench she asks where from here shall
    we go

in 3 years when she completes her work in *afrique* she'll
    want a baby

i always want to have child with the man i love
she sings, spread frog-like & adoring
my precision at inserting
another finger

she admits to never having enjoyed sex before
until now (with you stupid)

again upstairs we fuck till we can't
remember what time we arrived or why we go anywhere

i can no longer afford to live in my country
but will follow this woman into the maw of surrender

in the dream i have completed my farewell tour
of western states and am wending my way
backwards

i am on a dock preparing to toss my cell phone
into the harbor   when it vibrates

she wants a letter of recommendation that says
she spent the year translating my book
into japanese

i have to remind her she didn't even finish
reading it & she laughs

didn't you know short of death & acts of defiance
against nature it's not finished
until the princess says

and even then
perhaps

coming back from ocean beach on the streetcar
the thick light of san francisco's
storied afternoons, we stop

across from the gas station where i'd fill up
for the trip to san jose to see my uncle's
family and sleep on the couch

jesus, 20 years

after viewing art all afternoon she returns to a previous
    theme to tell me in broad strokes

her teaching on okinawa—drinking *sake* with students
    who suddenly got rough

undressing her, not to mention fighting with fists—*i failed*
    she says. *that was my 1st failure*

the next day abandoning her post because her students
    could not look at her with respect

that's from drinking she admits
i hold her in my arms—and whisper

okinawa means rope
in the offing, enough
to hang yrself

asuko let us bear witness to ourselves with thunder
& hemorrhage on the bottom

on new year's eve we change hotels when
there's a commotion next door

a couple going at it, the usual   the man hollers
and a door slams

asuko complains she can't sleep so i step out
to investigate like i know what to do

and find the couple embracing in the hall, the air
smelly of socks & bad whiskey

it's quiet & i don't think they see me
and besides they wouldn't care

when we make love asuko stops in mid
cry to ask if she's too loud

no i assure her   but it's too late
she will never cry in my arms again

asuko sends me books that resist description
each one takes me deeper down stairwells
to an underground vault

meanwhile she catalogs photos she's taken
on telegraph hill in her journal
how methodical

from michelle tea's horoscope in the bay guardian
(edited)   1-1-06

>scorpio you have to let go of something
and what you end up saying goodbye to
might be pretty frigging monumental
so we beg you to stay really checked in
with yourself   there are things that
absolutely need to be dealt with
right now

on the night of the 6th day i announce
it won't work   i do not relish the last chapter
of my life in dread

at midnight i rise from bed when my heart acts up

the point comes where you have to decide
to write this or continue
to live

in the morning we go out with hurt feelings
& order newspapers & coffee
i ask about her quote friend unquote
speaker of 7 languages who lives in magazines—
in short, made for her

but she's pissed off—so what it's because
she loves him, i argue

no it's because my questions have made her angry
at him

i explain for the thousandth time my concern
for our chances of success

so what do you want to do, she asks
let me think

call it denial
that we choose to make our monkey music
in a room high up while we wait to catch our planes

our defiance against the odds

on the night of the 5th day we discuss protocol in public
      places   it's difficult for her to hold eye contact
while eating

over coffee & cigarettes, ok but not dinner
important that people not get too explicit an idea
we're together   it is a matter
of *dousa,* motion or manners

i feel the need to remind her she's just pinched
my ass on market st.
                      oh she laughs
that's different

by morning i've thought it over & decide protocol
is for actors and explain
that *auteurs* who improvise
resist yelling "cut" at scene's end

but keep the cameras running

asuko, only when actors have nothing to say can we get
      the truth   & burst the straps
of the straitjacket called
relationship

but for you i hereby consent to avert
my gaze in public places
                      for you
will i walk backward eyes
closed & my hands
above my head and call it
bunraku

for you will i go weeks the width & height of honshu
and count the hours

not good news being announced in japan today
she writes

a story about ghosts from world war II

well i go to the mountain now   have a good life
there   please dress warmly
in cold places   asuko

her last email to me   after 2 ½ months
no word   & not enough forgotten

one night last week in a dream she came
yuurei, a princess in ghost mask

who froze my eyes   i woke up gasping   jesus
she's committed suicide on "the mountain"
and i will never know

10 days total contact in the flesh
not including the flush of emails between us

every affair its lexicon   ours
includes the words *ever, want, meditation
paris,* and oh yes, *love*

i'm thinking of the bird in *la gare du nord*
fluttering madly in search of a chirping
cell phone

like an old attorney once said: having an affair
online is like seeing a very bad psychiatrist

her father a maoist once involved in the cause
of the red army in the 60s, in fact
defended them in court

her grandfather upon his retirement
as magistrate, became an agent
of the secret police

and investigated his son until
ordering his arrest for collaboration
with the anti-imperialist brigade

thus asuko is adamant
in her refusal to discuss politics
except to lament that all of asia hates her

in the house of pluto we are each suspicious of the other's
> unleashed power

but what else can two scorpios do when they hit town
from opposite ends of the earth

we unite forever, part ways forever, take no prisoners
forever

religion=sex, trees stretched by gusts   death a ghost
of the inexpressible

according to *Love Signs:* "The physical expression of their
> love
has about it a haunting & indefinable nuance, which
> may elude them on a conscious level...."

we have spent our lives searching   no further frontier
> can withstand the bald rain in our hearts

"The mutual sensitivity & deep wells of need they
> both possess cause their lovemaking to be an
> extraordinary source of fulfillment...."

alone in my body a moon   no metaphor or symbology
for such emptiness is sublime

underline this: "She is not as aloof & unmoved as her
    silences indicate."

recall the character
heiki: coolness, unconcern, indifference

i said: yr solitude is so old no matter how fiercely i hold
    you

i'm aware of how much i've lived, i wrote
you realize how much you haven't

absence is essential. intimacy craves separation
in extremis: death

we need a break from each other every 10 days 10
    thousand years, aeons

she makes lists of all her books so she doesn't buy one
she already owns

i remark about her bibliomania and add
that i want to make love on a floor of open books

(silence)   have i offended you
oui

the key to our overwhelming difficulty says the book:
forgiveness

soul sick, floating too long
on theory, music, zen & paris
chants d'amour

in winter i walk past the house
where heloise met abelard
and opened her notebook

on the morning of dec. 25th i awoke
fed the cat, ran a bath and knew
it was over

traveling to distant places you recall the feeling
after you've decided to leave the city
where you live with a ticket out

that the final week or month on the job, in bed or
in restaurants before departure

is so sweet it's enough to make you almost reconsider
notice i said *almost*

such is our passage over the "hump"
into burma where prisoners
who lost at cards jumped
without a chute

we trust we will be indicted for war crimes
for seeking another country

so many misadventures mourned my father
what a shame his son could not
learn
      but i am not afraid to suffer

our passage long purchased   without our knowledge
prior to departure nothing in the universe
is without urgency

in the words of the chef at chez bertrand
enjoy!

in paris she'd wanted to touch my energy, she sd
the time we three went to cinema odeon
at midnight to see

les demons de la liberte, par jules dassin
with burt (the dog) lancaster
& sister yvonne

my friend jack always spoke in subtitles
the better to practice his french
and appear nightly

i do not speak during films, i do not hold
hands or nibble *madeleines*
to interrupt our trance

so that is what she meant, that explains
her going out to find a cab

at 3 a.m. to tell her boyfriend, *non*
it is really no use to go on

her sister in real life studies dietetics & works
in pharmaceuticals in aichi nagoya

stronger than asuko she scolds the older one
for her vision of the future

stronger than their mother and queen of the hive
she remains the "pretty one"

suddenly she shows up weeping, staying 3 nights
after an "argument" with her husband

asuko sleeps on the couch while mother & sister
drink whiskey before the tv

in december asuko & her mother will take the train
to tokoku to visit the grave of her father

they fear much snow in northern honshu
esp. serious with asuko's delicate health since africa

the attached photo is a snowman with head tapered
like a buddha—perfectly sculpted

surrounded by you, she writes, *i am happy always
and can do anything*

it does not occur to me that it requires hours
of rehearsal for her merely to ask if i've arrived

she's grateful for our wonder of 3 days
in paris & explains

that her character is so strange it may be
difficult to believe i am missed

apologizing for her broken english
she proposes a rendezvous

but adds: if you don't feel you love me
it will be not good for us

i always want to touch yr hair
& to kiss you, she writes

je t'aime, mon prince. a bientot, asuko

p.s. if you don't want to see me i will join
the nuns & help clean people's houses

in japan exists a religious order of 200 men & women
    who live very simply in families, run their gardens
    & farms

& buzz around town visiting people who are sick or
    otherwise incapable of caring for themselves

they come right in & clean the whole house
they do all the washing & clean out
the toilets   and then they just
disappear, sd asuko
lighting her last cigarette

topics that came up for discussion the morning after:

who you are is what you cut out of newspapers

the great thing about reading instead of singing
you don't have to tell the band
what key

the great thing about the blues you can go
to the can & come back
& it's still there

from paris i might not come back alive
then come back dead. *ha,* either way
it's 1 bedroom w/heat

delight in 1 thing overlapped
with memory: sweetness
of cream centered chocolates
a radio ballgame & searing
red meat. lena horne
in rags, looking stern

that's america to me

kerouac said this life was a dream that's
already over

like dead stars whole galaxies just beginning
to appear

not to mention my 1st night's sleep
alone—sweet enough to wake up & taste

no greater pleasure than to wake up
with yr sheets undisturbed

at dawn i rise, urinate & start the coffee
at last there is so much a man can do

my professional adjusts our last session to ask
why i'm going

she means paris but won't say it in so many words

for a cup of coffee, what else

have i studied the language she asks
non
      but the best method i've heard of
is to lay up with a beautiful woman
a native preferably

so that's the plan. *oui*

and now i'm holed up at the *hotel les argonautes*
in sainte chappelle with st. augustine's
confessions

and don't laugh it's really fucked me up

asuko leads me on tours of temples in kyoto, osaka
& nara   i wait outside in the rain
while limos line up purring

burn it down i chant, subscriber
to no doctrine
suzuki shosan sd to put a match to things
& study death

shi ni narau that's what i have done
with all my love   especially
my sex as signature

our death will leave us both
exhausted
              as for me
just burn my smelly ass & toss it
over the fantail

now for that cup of coffee in a smoky shop
that sells *manga* by the pound

she begged me please to change my departure back
as we agreed upon   and not to leave early

without saying if i go it will prove her failure to hold me,
    her deficiency as a lover

next she came to my room, undressed, got on the bed &
    said   you want me change yr ticket to tuesday

we made love and fell asleep for 3 months
the rest is history   world war II came & went without
incident

in the dream we drove to gifu to stay at the house her
    mother used to forage wild plants for medicine

we slept on the porch and made love by moonlight, and
    all my days were spent adoring bamboo

the golden relic exists, says the koan
"Foaming billows sweep the sky. Where can you put
    it?
No, nowhere!"*

*Albert Low, Case #55
of the Hekiganroku: *Alive or Dead*

awakened by rain at 4 a.m
huge splashes on stone:
makes me a woman

now will they know what i mean

why i move to distant cities & its ponderous effects...
there is a word i cannot name for looking
backwards & finding nothing

it is time in my life to put all such karma into books—
as storage & delivery

print on demand a means of traveling *sans* texts, notes
& boxes of manuscripts

makes it possible to enter cities with pen & a change
of underwear   monastic, plain
& fervent

not to mention my wish to avoid the temptation of exile
again to fix up the place *the way you like it* & discover
i can't work there

death is always the next door
& is an artist's lover

look up *incontinence* to be certain:
failure to control urges, esp. in matters of sex
extravagance

thus my failure to control said desire
has made me dirty: our intimacy
stained by secrets

our last night late from a sushi house in gifu
i decline even water and she
thinking me rude

at home friends are building cabins in the mountains—
for the day my country
"shits the bed" as quoted

i can't go another night up a mountain in the dark
climbing stairs   ashamed of soiling the sheets
i hide the evidence

longitude north by northwest
the love hotel dreamt of in kobe as a joke
unattempted

god honors not regularity & incontinence
merely a hint of the unknowable   besides
all flesh is shit in the end

tomorrow i will leave early to catch a plane
and take my 1st good crap
at the airport at chubu

that year at gifu i could only be induced to return
if i could teach cloud watching

to americans: to see them roll in spilling of news
from deep down

walking my shadow in the late afternoon
& not having to be anywhere
but where you are

and my beloved bamboo leeward in its glittering
such is the life in my heart i lost

asuko an orphan over & over cannot break out of the
    configuration
of three—required to feel secure
such as we are

asuko, i, and the man recovering from wounds in
    belgrade, always the korean or somebody else

as for me, my being, my being here & my being home in
    the mind without struggle

that we will always be as shadows to each other only
    makes me crave her more

due to the 14 hr difference according to the watch
she sent me with the book
on *noh*

asuko emails to tell me that pittsburgh lost
to the mets last night before
i swear the game's been played

her interest in the outcome esp. keen
as the losing pitcher
once played for yokohama

sometimes you press at just the right angle
with just the right circumflex
and all is revealed

late at night in my home town touching myself
on the cot in the garage
while wind rattles the trees

then rain at once so sweet
it breathes like a woman too good
to be true

asuko comes & shows you—*yes*
you think, i don't know if i can
handle this

now listen to me she says you
can handle it, believe me
you can handle it

on the 20th day of the 2nd month (lunar) 1387
at age 61 (my age as written)
bassui a monk

said: *Look straight ahead. What's there?*
　　　If you see it as it is
　　　You will never err.

repeated it & died

seeing it as it is—that's always been my problem
just as i've always known it
but was afraid

asuko beside me once asked for a cigarette
in french, and for lack of a better word
i said yes

i forgot i don't even smoke

like jack nicholson in *the two jakes* (1990)
said to the daughter of faye
dunaway when she comes on
to him: "that's yr problem

you don't know who you're kidding"

it seems there was a phone call though no one knows
who took it as it's after 1958

and everyone's asleep after midnight

my father says it was my mother and she's coming home
tomorrow explanation to follow   she's dead
of course, i thought you knew   that morning
in january—as much as we've been told

but things change, he means, there's been a change
in plans listen

yr mother didn't die exactly as reported, or rather she did
    but something happened or

so straighten up the house   she'll be here
and there won't be time

as a family we skip breakfast skip lunch   we have
    brushed our teeth & bathed   and are waiting

in our communion suits with our hands folded   dad
has gone to pick her up downtown

she will not be like herself we are warned and will not
feel like playing   do not yell or make loud noises

we promise and are sure to be peeking out the windows
    when they pull up in the chevy

dad with her luggage says look who's here
when she enters pale & crazy

touches the curtains & exclaims dreamily how good
to be back   and we shout to interview her

about her adventures but are urged back to our rooms
to be summoned later

i met daigu in a book called *japanese death poems*
(jisei) a collection of haiku & waka
written by monks before dying

daigu had quit the monastery and lived
"in the mountains"—a euphemism
for checking out of this hotel

daigu was known to like his *sake*—not
total inebriation per se, but
sipped for the sake of maintenance

he did not allow it to hamper his flow
of insults while suffering visitors who flocked
because he was "eccentric"

he had a reputation for enjoying the intimacy
of women and was regarded as unreliable
in fact *daigu* means "great fool"
                                                this monk
is bound in chains of ignorance and lust, he wrote
He is not able to follow the way of the Buddha
As his name is, so is he—

before his death he wrote a poem praising himself
as "unique in his generation"
                                    kitsu! mac
   i love this monk
                  is it too late to write
& tell her there's a place on this earth for guys like me

reasons to marry and reasons not to marry by geoff peterson

neat japanese stuff incl. kanji. noh zen—we fight alot—possible publication in japan—sex is risky w/o birth control—she can't use b.c. except condoms—sex is good/great—needy, requires much attention—very sensitive to my needs/moods—she's often arbitrary, crazy, inconsistent—she has her own $—costly (x2)—better diet/reg. meals—does not travel well in wilderness & road trips—she likes baseball—poor health, smoker—she turns me on to films & books—wishes to live here & buy a house—we're both scorpios—she's a dragon i'm a dog—disapproves of my behavior—she can be wise & thoughtful—says very hurtful things to me—she's savvy with computers—she's controlling—has a tender relationship with the cat—she wants to have a child & keep it—she "knows" certain things—age difference—prayer & meditation—she's argumentative "no, geoff" & won't listen—
honesty, integrity?—i never know the truth about the woman, never get to the answers: *who is she*

but she likes baseball the sex
splashed with hiragana
& we fight alot

i am a man and a man as only a man knows
is god in the flesh: that
is the basis of our argument

asuko i can only promise everything broken that roaring
    in the hall the heart marching toward bataan

indulge me a sip of brandy a drag off an untamed cigarette
    my love is slight

a hair clipping sealed in money   reams of lost connections
    & missed departures by seconds excuse me

to take a message or answer a call of nature i have
    always loved you but cannot be with you hands
    folded in thanks

how can i make you see the weeks & months of nothing
    but poems & coffee cups i am not afraid to be
    without you

asuko my love for you is summoned because you have
    no one thus i have come to be had

this afternoon i caught a breeze off the river
i never knew in all my struggle
it could be like this

recall how you always say *sorry, so sorry, please*—
but it is i who beg forgiveness

for my rages, lies about women, spending
yr money, deserting you in my country
& yours

for words hanging in traffic   frequent
lapses of attention, neglecting you in bed
my losing our cat not once, twice
the last time the last

the big moon of wyoming is humming with summer's
    last breath

here where the dust whirls up today
in times gone by was a sprawling sea
wrote han shan

add thunder to the rumors of a war once passed this way,
    took what it wanted & moved on

followed by the last rain of the empire
what's the reason to go on living sd lincoln

when you're old the last great pleasure is crying

to honor her place we honor the idea this is happening
    at all

look out—it means nothing but trouble
the story demands

for instance this hotel in words weighted like spinoza
chuang tzu or djuna barnes

or consider the lost book of the pentateuch
his gaze upon us
after he's brought us
to a river

consider this an interview for the job of going on
without me

americans are so serious & sad
sd phillip whalen
back when it meant something

i have the pictures she sent in the mail:
the island's gold cliffs in the dark
the boats in the channel

between us & china a marriage of light & wave
only available at the end

what held me back that night my bowels closed
tighter than rock

& what still binds me to my misery over water
by the time we leave this world
all is broken

shanti shanti groaneth the poem i read
to the old nun in her sleep
inside the padding

man & woman we want different things

but she says what she wants is natural & remains for
    all time

it's fixed says she—what men & women both want

so i must not love her enough or i would want—that is
what she wants   being as it's natural

& she unable to help herself having fallen for a savage

listen baby we don't need to call up any buddhas with
    our prayers they got our number

you fucking crazy bitch
kitsu!

she said in tokyo where she'd gone to school
she watched a movie with her mother

& the american said "pussy"

asuko the only one in the audience to laugh

i sd i loved to hear her happy and meant it
& she said thank you

tonight we kiss over the telephone
& whisper goodnight

since agreeing to conduct this affair via satellite
i've enlisted with boat people, undocumented
& displaced persons seeking sanctuary
lovers on the run from pressures
from without

women stealing to feed their babies
stalking the wounded to slaughter, that is
the old law before the books

lives who with each breath
run their cups against the rusted bars

i told her at 61 yrs i look up to no man
and she downcast
coming from a family of short people

i tell about a meditation group i've joined
& she interrupts to say she's glad
i'll be happy

but we cannot be together   translation:
she's found a new boyfriend

i love how women get that ice cold infusion
of clarity at the end

23/04/07
breakup #33

i'm getting real tired of having this conversation over
& over, i'm through

if that's what you want   why

that's what i want because we go around & around with
      this & get nowhere

i don't understand how you cannot help but see
what's going on the choices you make
scare me

you call it being japanese but it's something else
believe me i know twisted, i twisted off
years before you

i've paid dues to meet you   but you
always change yr mind   you tell a different version of
      what's happened when i need a straight answer

you can't give me a straight answer

what is a straight answer

we touch down 30 years after the dream called
okinawa (i still have the ticket)

all things japanese leave me happy & desolate
sorry in french leaves one seasick

because of you i have completed the circle
of that life

now let us move along the rim of white light
without guides

in nara tonight i lie awake in tanizaki's room
to be inspired

instead i live the story
of someone with delicate hands
forgive me i whisper

i have always lied telling the truth

she's emailed to say she owes her mother money to fix
the summer home above gifu

she will work in town brewing gourmet coffee
and get by on tips from salarymen

this will take years, she says, more or less depending
on living costs & the price of gasoline

i get the picture: she wants me to move
in with her & study bamboo in the mountains

alas we too successfully adjust to the world   in the
    words of yogi berra: *count me out*

2 years later say the titles: what shadow in the spotlight
    of this drama made me utter those words—

alone at a window in a fogbound city i remain wounded
    by nameless beasts of the sea

in fact i never felt enough all at once to say it
what is missing that best wears the mask
called asuko

kokoro, the heart of things
what was it then about you & me you knew
all my life

defective of heart to sustain us
too delicate to meet you at a bus stop
correct change in hand

with neither talent nor the desire to be princely
there is nothing to sing, nothing
to say that changes us

it's no longer the horizon but the shore inside
where language exists
for what is & was & shall be

and if there's a way to learn it so help me i too
was raised by a grandmother

this is the skinny the lowdown where it hurts
before we met i was already
inconsolable

one day in another year our cat *hang-ets* will show up
in the hall by the mailboxes

and residents will pass her on the staircase & assume
she was never lost   asuko-san,

you taught me the name means half moon
drawing the character for who we are

neko the auspicious character for cat
& *bake-neko*, the goblin cat

in the shadows between the buildings on yr street
i sing of the dead & missing

and know it is i who have joined their ranks
and you who have always lived there

asuko writes what she told me
in paris that an ex-boyfriend thought of having a family
    thus she moved

to *afrique* & worked beside him   *he understood well*
his commitments, she says   *when i saw him*
in sept. he told me that after he'd met me
he had not had any other woman

resided 9 months (black africa: senegal, mali) & north
    africa (morroq, algeria) before becoming sick

in hospital a doctor who knows endemic diseases came
to me with news of infection & treated my ulcers
as one physician channels another
on the outskirts of dakar

by 8 a.m. heat enough to drive you rabid
clawing out of yrself   delirious
heat to kill without yr breaking a sweat
endless flies   the center of town
unsafe for whites she sd
open yr eyes

shootings & rapes & rumors
less than worthy for the papers
even an asian takes a cab head down doors locked
& to buy what a woman needs, *impossible*

i set my thumbs along her spine & draw the shoulders
backwards   ahh, *nekoze* a cat's back
and touch her nostrils with the scent of *jilal*

i recommend a cessation of smoking
and a cutback in alcohol
a rigorous schedule of meditation exercise sleep
& stretching for posture

the results of hiv tests pending   *but i thought perhaps
i could have been exposed since then,* she adds
without explanation

so i will seek testing for sida *before i come to the u.s.
though it takes 3 months as you know*

thus we come to history in the black skin of another
in strips & tatters
on the horizon the signs
red with warning inviting us to the fruits of one life
such as they are

*really i have been with no one but you ever since   is this
        the information you wanted i hope
        naked*

in the shade at 112 & the tamarinds sag on the branch:
        in a dream it came to me like opening a fist
& finding chocolate, she is not
in japan but at the place she has found the most
to lose
i have scheduled my shots & booked
my ticket—1 way

let's see if i can talk my way out of that

asuko in the lateness of life wakes up without a father
& must respect her body

toilet, bath, feeding   unbroken sleep   she is not
to be confused with her performing
these rites   that is why

i love her, why i return and cannot go forward
as i told the old nun in the convent
she has no one

maybe this explains her intense pursuit
of *couvades* the brotherhoods
that comprise her geography

today i hang the photos i've taken down
and listen to flies as the sound
my cock makes dashing this off
in sumi-e to the next world

what will you do asks my therapist
will you walk the plank as the next step in yr life
remove the blindfold

buddha's fire sermon
defines our craving as sheer exhaust
of emptiness

speed the measure, juggernaut
its denoument   modern
desolation if you will

its twilight will break yr heart

in conversation with my therapist at an ashram in upstate
poughkeepsie my concern about love being social

explains the power of japanese legend, my
obsession with its *shi* the poem
itself, as in

kore wa watashino okinirino shi desu:
"this is my favorite poem"
by asano akiko but
unable to recite it without notes

at 62 nervous about dementia
& unqualified to explore the hauntings
of doomed principles

i hereby submit the way to go into love—all at once
spread out like a rearrangement
of the senses to be willing to check out
of the cage called wisdom
with none of yr belongings but each other
grip to grip

stretching the last line to infinity   that is to be here
& to know *i am god*

he says go forth there is nothing to fear of yr own path
of course there is no path no you
& love   what is that

but a rumor of the poem that desires to begin

once more enters the kimono girl & steps
down the causeway

in the music's fervor
such mystery compacted at this depth

again forgetting to breathe
i wake up gasping

oh yes, this life

i'm writing in a cafe where i can't think because the
    music's bent on destruction but

i told tom b. it's my 2nd day here & i'm sucking oxygen
through a straw
fiery thoughts non-stop

today bound for coffee & a leftover Times to check for
    jobs....
but stop for a dose of a/c at little tokyo's branch
library & check my mail

but the line's endless and everything's as fake
as modern man permits
so go back where they keep the good stuff
japanese

lit. in translation & pick out
Ukiyo: Stories of the "Floating World" of Postwar Japan

and fall upon "The Crane That Cannot Come Back"
by Seto Nanako, published by UNESCO
its Committee for World Memory

treated for radiation sickness it's a diary of her last year
    1958
    oh god let me live
and in peace she writes to the bell's tolling
how hateful to be tried by god

her illness reminds me of asuko's assumptions: headache
    cough   anxiety   stomach disorders   sore
throat
ringing in the ears
anemia   exhaustion   liver pain
stiffness   backache
persistent fever

& loneliness so intense it keeps her awake
i inherit from my mother
as written

at the hospital *such utter loneliness* when they come
for her roommate & adds
i cannot…live long since i am a broken person

daughter mami to start kindergarden: makes her so
    happy when she comes to visit   but at departure
    unspeakable sorrow

hiromi her brother, sullen, dares not show emotion
a troubled child   *we are all black sheep*
she laments   god *that's me*

now i know why she didn't want us to see her at the end
    that same year oh mom

here i sit all afternoon in the little tokyo branch
to read 16 pages

the kinkaid hotel in downtown los angeles
affordably fireproof says the ad

all the snoring people curled tonight in the cracks
of the foundation

i'm making conversation with an old resident
who shows me where to look
for clean towels

a woman who has not cried wet tears
in 50 years
and endures panic in bed

*i've lived my life but you--what are you trying to throw
away*   i don't know as i do not have a home she says
i know

once i heard a man say you can see it coming
but don't have the power to stop it
or get out of the way

then it's over   that other life
and you can't get it back but take the steps
underwater

someone said time was invented so that everything didn't
         happen at once   outside
motocycles peel away from the music's jukebox
& across the street drunken salarymen
howl at streetlights
then go home with women

asuko asuko
the theme on which i've pinned my last wild ride
is gone

& i will never outgrow my bourgeois pity
for myself in the name of others

3 flies hover above the bed in the corner room on the 5th
    floor of this hotel

i'm suspicious as they never land or make a sound

maybe they're not flies but floaters on the eyes or some
    deep neurological phenomenon known to precede
    a stroke

should i call an amulance or tell myself all will be fine
& lie in my own shit

on the wall's a faded print of a harbor to some celestial
city   freighters like 1940 steaming down a fabulous
east river

in the beginning was new york & my whole life
cloud-written   while asuko's grandparents
shoveled ashes
          i could go on
while the ceiling unravels to unveil a *demimonde*
lit by spiders

as for the picture hanging in this 1 room out of a million
    units that range across the night there is no
    connection

asuko i went to sfMOMA again without you & saw the
>   kahlo exhibit   the *auto retrato con moros* (1943)

it made me think of you—yr hairline & yr love of monkeys
>   *ken'en no naka*, you said, a dog & monkey
relationship—that's us

in my last dream i learned how to leave you   farewell
as understood, walking to the bus in fog

i imagine turning to frida posing with her bleeding cunt
>   to argue about art & mutability *the man i love
does not want me* she rages

sin esperanza says the guide in his intro to her later
>   works
after "love embrace of the universe"
no hope for us but desire
empty in its place

no hope for those who eat their children or count
>   themselves out   no hope
as pre-condition for birth

all week without fog i shoot pictures of pigeons in open
     windows 1 or 2 nesting

then dozens on a roof
or what about the hundreds in the airshaft all spiraling
     out of control into new life forms:

milkmen, window washers
karate instructors
you

in an empty movie theatre being screamed at
by previews from the heart
of darkness i saw it

what i'd come all this way for

all this life seeking the mad dragon of search
& destroy but instead
addressing her priestess in seaweed
& an ancient mask

sensei of the horizon she called me   translated

means one never content not being elsewhere
a deep horrible & debilitating
condition sd a friend who suffers

now that she left me alone how will i live, where
will i go and who will i be so it matters

the text offers little to suggest that the answer to that
& other questions is to enter the abyss

taeru means to cease, to die out, to end, at last
to be cut off

composed 2-09-08
longitude 122° west

in los angeles i stop at a broadway watch shop to buy
a leather strap: so far so good

smartly the japanese proprietor
comes from behind the counter to help

after he successfully matches a band in stock
with mine, it's time to inquire
about price

$24 he quotes
twenty-four dol-lars the watch
isn't worth half that

but without another word his attention turns
to the next customer

there is nothing to be continued between us
what is left to do
but walk out

that's the difference between asuko & me

my father went to the pacific in world war 2
thinking life & death
are different

that explains his wonder at kamikazes
& clasping his unborn children to himself
for fear they'd perish

i told her what i love about japan is how everything's
clean   as maintenance workers
are not viewed as are janitors in america

but as a most honorable elevated cadre
of professionals   and she sd

thank you because we in japan are most proud
of that   and i said
i know

in bed toward the end i told her let's make love
without the back story
for a change

that is love without the design
for living we're supposed to swallow but naked
instead be here

then what's the point she said   meaning what's the point
    of doing this our anything
for that matter
        that's the point
i said: *saigo* defined as last, the end
once, as in once upon a time or that
was the last time i saw her

at the end she tightened & lifted right off the bed staring
    into my eyes

we were never that close again

asuko i'm sad & tender & full of tears
having drafted a poem about missing the dead
     here i am—

inside a room in the rain at the end of a hall
is a tv talking

rooms to rent is becoming next to impossible
& deep down i'm too old for women

the day we pulled the plug on my friend i walked out
possessed of nothing
all the cities numb, the juice
gone the salt gone the chops
gnawed to the bone

8 years and there's no place left to drive
the dead send their best & desire we go on
without them

i remain by the phone without hope

asuko i can no longer help myself matter
beyond my fingers a roaring
in the trees, the last light
rushing into the grapes

postscript: puerto vallarta
14/9/08

lunes i move into the studio at pino suarez
 ½ block
from the pacific
with coffee pot & cable

single sober & full of shit
with 30 days to enter the world's wound
i'll go under & come up
hands outstretched

on shore a bronze sculpture of a male
& female presumably, together
watching the parade
                    in the afternoon it burns
to touch their bodies

i am a bronze body
at night elegant women approach me   all
i can say is i have no money

remember dick & liz coming down in '64
on the set of *Iguana*
with ava & the cabana boys
tennessee drunk & fighting for his scenes

and now me at the very edge:
it is the rainy season
& china is out there

my bowels are telling me it's no use: yr thinking is out
to destroy you so i'll make it clear

how long will it take to recognize you cannot repeat
cannot shit if she's within a hundred miles

get out of the car you heard me get out
& make that plane

the big one marked OUTOUTOUT OUT
or TOUT TOUT in french i can't tell
sayonara & thanks for flying
 united

now go write yr fucking poems   oh
i forgot—they aren't poems
but texts, i stand corrected

god what is the matter with me
there is a beautiful woman who works in the creperie
that i wish to get next to

i want to say it's strange
having hauled my weight across galaxies
to know love

but i'm afraid of her telling her family & their laughing
& my being challenged to announce
my intentions

& breaking down over dinner overwhelmed by sheer
tonnage of longing

everything in my life is broken
i offer her nothing
but the need to be mended

but i say none of it not one word or soulful look
because asuko dwells
at depth

& cannot breathe

when we first met in paris, i mean before we spent
our night together in the marais

she was always saying *i'm sorry* this/*i'm sorry* that
for what i don't know   in english
i'd insist

she'd never answer but she knew   it upset me
to think i showed dissatisfaction, i mean
with what she knew i didn't

it didn't occur to me till months later that it meant
i love you

you cannot look after her if you are always worried
about yrself, says a voice

thus the problem: too much beside her makes me
restless

i am the sea, she the island
there are so many fish
strange to her

women as gift always form-fitting me
to earth, made the world
eased into   but she

lifts me out of form & abolishes me
to air

these & other comments received courtesy of ravel's
pavanne   long after the fact

someday i'll come back and stop for chinese at a place
in an alley without name & order something with garlic
    sauce

and invite the attention of the owner's daughter who
    waits tables and gives me extras with my meal
    including

bags of fortune cookies which i'll read alone in the park
frantically adrift in the fog's text

that i'll call you damn the cost as a desperate medicine
to get past the nights making the rounds of our old
circuit like a guard of the heart *coptis japonica* the root
of all medicine says han shan, advising you mix
yr tonic with garlic to ease the going down

do you need to remind me that i have written this over
& over many times

by the calendar the affair lasted a total of 710 days
tokyo time

number of days spent together in the flesh: 99

the days we were separated by oceans were productive

33 of the 99 together
spectacular

the remaining can only be left to the visceral
 imagination

drama & desire #2 says i'm staying with a physician (asian) & his family in their modern designer home on the outskirts of arizona

sleeping on living room floor   two children (sons) upstairs & a wife

in the morning comes a call from asuko who says by the way   traveling east we're scheduled to arrive los angeles, sister city of nagoya

i suspect she's accompanied by her mother or sister & suggest i catch a flight and be there same day   asuko can be less than cordial when a voice comes on & says so far this call is being monitored & costs $70

billed to the doctor's landline   i say hang up i'll call you back on my cell, but as i fumble with my backpack it comes out all broken & deranged

drama & desire, cont.

in this version i fly out & meet her at the airport or hotel downtown
she's alone in a galaxy of products and wears new clothes
i have bought a ring & offer a fitting, proposal of marriage, etc
but she says please

i tell her it's too late i have spent the money and am in debt having lost everything, & beg her come back and begin to assemble ingredients to make a scene, mindful of obsession as the expressive form of emotional blockage, of the past shut off & the future unthinkable

when a young immaculately dressed japanese or korean guy arrives and is introduced as her husband

i get up, dust myself off, bow appropriately, receive his card: so, it's you

commentary: it's clear how this "ending" is expressive of our separate karmas as invoked by the material referred to above as drama & desire

asuko moves on, that's the point—with husband, her life i its author having written stay back both having obtained

out of expediancy: intimacy/solitude   the need
to believe it, the divide in my heart according to legend
as deep as the ocean trench

textes a mallarme

stephane mallarme 1842-98 held his salon on tuesdays
a paris
        examine the poem
"un coup de des jamais n'abolera le hazard" (a throw
of the dice will never abolish chance)
                                    foreshadows
playfulness of typeface in *poesie contemporaines*
see **les poemes concrete**

did you know he made his living teaching english

at the same time his theories parallel those of abstract
impressionists

a forebear of the *symbolistes* he studied under
baudelaire: the transcendental world
suggested by use of ellipses & ambiguous
sentence structure this, quote/unquote
creates a pervasive sense of the mystery
of everyday objects—
les objets mistere

pour example undress a banana, whose leathery strips
beneath the skin tip to tip
in biopsy

how many are required to peel until sd banana
itself is nothing   now can you detect
seeds of fascism in his method
                                    in praise
of obscurity & mystery, *poesie* he said
should approach the abstraction *de la musique*

in attendance at the man's tuesday salons
verlaine & valery but no rimbaud

to discuss *herodiade* (1869) *l'apres-midi
d'un faune* (1876) see debussy, claude
all the cats who cooked up *musique serie*
sheer ambience

inspired ravel's *trois poemes de stephane mallarme*
    (1913)
darius milhaud's *chansons
bas de stephane mallarme* (1917)
& pierre boulez's *pli selonpli* (1957-62)
                                              not to
    mention
man ray's last film *les mysteres du chateau du de*

he translated "the raven" for god's sake
(illustrated by edouard monet)
& saw to it that valery received the gospel
"according to *moi*"

& he made his living teaching english teaching english
les mots anglais (1878)
lest we forget

as did soseki natsume of the meiji period   who soon
quit to write for the *shimbun*
& a masterpiece *ten nights of dreams*   (witness his
    face
on 1000 yen banknotes)

finally what feature distinguishes mallarme for asuko
is his notion of form as precursor
of *hypertext*   not to mention

the impossibility of translating his work into english
thus i remain
smitten

mallarme, cont.

the poem "le apparition" reminds me that you do not need to be astute in *francaise* to recognize there are poets who work the day shift and those who work the night

Le Apparition

La lune s'attristait. Des seraphins en pleurs
Revant, l'arche taux doigts, dans le calme des fleurs
Vaporeuses, tiraient de mourantes violes
De blanc sanglots glissant sur l'azur des corolles.
--C'etait le jour beni de ton premier baiser.
Ma songerie aimant a me martyriser
S'enivrait savamment du parfum de tristesse
Que meme sans regret et sans deboire laisse
La cueillaison d'un Reve au cœur qui la cueilli.
J'errais donc, loeil rive sur le pave vieilli
Quand avec du soleil aux cheveux, dans la rue
Et dans le soir, tu m'es en riant apparve
Et j'ai cru voix la fee du chapeau de charte
Qui jadis sur mes beaux sommeels d'enfant gate
Passait, laissant toujours de ses mains mal fermees
Neiger de blancs bouquets d'etoiles parfumees

                              --stephane mallarme

toutou: finally; in the end; after all

by resorting to these texts i remained enthrall to the
 affair for a year after its demise

i wanted to feel it utterly, beyond proportion, & to land
 at an unnamed spot

whether i succeeded in that i leave to you, as my life
is none of my business

the texts here are in order of their composition, rather
 than in any thematic or narrative order

as it's possible that the sequence of creation follows a
 logic unknown to us but barely discernible in a
 specific traction of the heart

i am convinced if a man persists in his commune with
 the authors
cited and the figures dwelling in the well of their texts
spirits will advance in the form of beautiful women
& to worship at the shrine of beautiful women
is to honor the gods

24-8-08

riding the sunset limited through the desert at dawn
bound for los angeles, the old haunts flying by

in the club car watching a long freight get the green light
with containers from asia

i can hear the words the day i called & caught her at
the airport in chubu bound for czechoslovakia

czech republic, she corrected. i don't care what
she calls it, i knew her purpose in going

but she argued that he was sick & needed help
meaning to cook his food & read to him

and i said *asuko you do not need to get on that plane
you do not have to do this   asuko, please*

*i love you & want to marry you   if you go i will have
lost you   please don't go*

and she asked what she should do and i said *go
to the agent, exchange yr ticket then go outside*

*hail a cab & go home   and when you get there
call this number*   and she did

and now a guy wants the cheese taken off his eggs
& demands to see where it says so in the book

a conductor has radio'd to request assistance   and i'm
drinking coffee

there's not a single drop of irony in any of this
i've even heard we're going to be on time

houhou: a method; a plan; a system

i saw the exhibition *drama & desire* at the asian art museum, 15 feb 2008 & began working on the early career of j. robert oppenheimer at the sf public library eleven days later

oppenheimer arrived at UC berkeley in august 1929 to teach quantum mechanics fall & winter semesters   it was there his life began to flower as it can only happen in california, and does

i wanted to combine my ideas about oppenheimer, which i had attempted to formulate with rob nilsson, filmmaker, on feb. 14 in berkeley

with my growing suspicion that i was never going to see again a woman from japan i'd been involved with for 2 years & counting

for weeks i struggled with the idea of oppenheimer & japan and his years at berkeley before his recruitment to head up the trinity project at alamagordo

i considered putting it on paper in the form of a film treatment—

oppenheimer at berkeley, sc. 1:
(buying a newspaper i descend the steps to the BART
        platform

>   voiceover: *oppenheimer is someone a certain kind of
>   man
>   chooses to feel close to. a man gifted in his field but
>   cursed
>   in a torturous, self-defeating way. sentenced to a
>   doomed love,*

> *conflicted re his own achievement, disappointed in his ultimate ambition....*

   this is how a man like that talks to himself

sc. 2: board the BART and ride it under the bay to berkeley

> voiceover: cell-phone conversation with japan. asuko asking
>   where to send my stuff—a novel, some poems, music—her
> voice breaking up)

etc.

finally in june i surrendered to the idea that lay behind the whole enterprise: the face of "asuko" appearing in dream as though a mask emerging from water....

old questions demanded new answers: for instance, could a marriage make it on sex & baseball   or did the odds favor rock n' roll & drugs *ipso facto*   not to mention literature

i repeat: the treatment never got written   or maybe this is it

i owe this to her & to everyone for the channel of world energy in desperate times i offer this text to george t. & geoff h. in appreciation for friendship that follows me always

to andy kirol, the man who introduced us, & who knew enough french to launch us on nervous water

to shaun & cornelia for food & technical support, and to chris weber for her encouragement & permission to quote her

special thanks to Rama for the photo image: *Masque-no* from wikipedia.com

to the *San Francisco Bay Guardian* for an excerpt from Michelle Tea's horoscope forecasts

to Kimiko Hahn for her dazzling *zuihitsu* named after Basho's *Narrow Road to the Interior* (New York: W.W. Norton & Co., 2006)

to the editors at Tuttle Publishing for quotes from *Japanese Death Poems*, compiled by Yoel Hoffmann (Tokyo: Tuttle Publishing, 1986)

to the editors at Grove Press for the Zeami quotes, the poem by Minamoto Shigeyuki & the excerpt from Heikiganroku, from the *Anthology of Japanese Literature* by Donald Keene (New York: Grove Press, 1955)

to the editors at HarperPerennial for quotes from *Linda Goodman's Love Signs* (New York: HarperCollins, 1992)

to the editors at Shambhala Publications for quotes from *Cold Mountain* poems by Han Shan, Burton Watson, trans. (Boston: Shambhala, 1992)

to the editors at Vanguard Press for excerpts from "The Crane that Cannot Come Back" by Seto Nanako, 1st published 1961 by the Committee for the Book, Hiroshima YMCA, 1961 & reprinted in
Ukiyo: Stories of the "Floating World" of postwar Japan, Jay Gluck, ed.

to the producers of the 2008 New York Metropolitan Opera production of *Dr. Atomic* by John Adams & Peter Sellars for quotations from the libretto

to the editors at Black Sparrow Press for the quote from Philip Whalen's novel *Imaginary Speeches for a Brazen Head* (Los Angeles: Black Sparrow Press, 1972)

to Emmett Lombard (faculty, Gannon University) for technical support

to Namiko Abe: japanese.guide@about.com for Japanese terms

& to the readers who read the manuscript and made suggestions

about the author

having recently returned to erie to consult with his youth

& having proposed to release the load that has brought him this far

& having rented a room and burning his clothes in the toilet

& having paid his rent by the week, the day, and now the hour

the author cannot cook if he is not hungry

if the radio plays a slow blues filling up with snow

& says the people who love you are killing you

the people who love you are dying faster than the snow

but the people you love you love you have not even met

are already dead